NANCY WARREN

TANGLES AND TREASON

VAMPIRE KNITTING CLUB PREQUEL

ISBN: ebook 978-1-990210-06-8

ISBN: paperback 978-1-998239-03-0

ISBN: digital PDF 978-1-990210-07-5

Ambleside Publishing

INTRODUCTION

In Elizabethan Oxford, Sir Rafe Crosyer is on a secret mission for the queen. He also wants to secure Constance's hand in marriage, not only for love but for her safety, for there are rumors afloat that Constance is a witch. But when he is attacked and left for dead, not only is his love in terrible danger, but also his queen. Unless he takes an unthinkable step...

If you have friends who love cozy paranormal mystery, please tell them about *The Vampire Knitting Club* and my other series...

The Vampire Knitting Club: Cornwall
The Vampire Book Club
The Great Witches Baking Show
The Village Flower Shop

Come join me in my private Facebook group where we talk about books, knitting, pets and life.
www.facebook.com/groups/NancyWarrenKnitwits

TANGLES AND TREASON

CHAPTER 1

Oxford, England. 1568

anger surrounded Rafe Crosyer, keeping his every sense alert as he strolled lazily down the High Street. Even in Oxford, spies were everywhere, and he knew the upcoming meeting was the most dangerous part of his secret mission.

But he was loyal to his queen and his country and if he could save the most fair Queen Elizabeth from a Spanish plot to kill her, then his life was well worth the forfeit.

He held the scented pomander to his nose, trying not so much to obliterate the stench of open sewers mixed with the anxious sweat of undergraduates, as to shield his face as his sharp gaze scanned ahead for danger.

He looked every inch the courtier, with his fine beaver hat, his lace neck ruff, black doublet, hose and fine wool breeches. But the sword hanging so nonchalantly at his side was sharp and true and his fashionable leather boots were well used to running toward a fight. Never away from one.

He passed Brasenose College, navigating around a group of boisterous students, and headed for The Bear Inn, his meeting place. His focus sharpened but Turl Street seemed quiet enough. A carriage lumbered down the road its wheels ringing on the cobblestones. A beggar with open sores beseeched him for a penny. He dropped the coin into the grimy open hand.

On impulse he turned not left, but right on Turl and detoured down Harrington Street. There was nothing here but a few cottages. Looking ahead, he viewed fields of grazing livestock and in the distance the dense forests of Wychwood where his own manor house was new built.

The cottage he sought was halfway down the street. Before walking up to the thick oak door, he cast a glance right and left to be certain he wasn't followed. He would not bring trouble to this house.

He knocked sharply on the door which was soon answered by a pretty maid. She dimpled when she saw him. "Bid you good day, sir. My mistress will be pleased to see you."

"Stay a moment, Betsy," he said, when she would have ushered him in. "Does your mistress entertain?"

She grew serious. "Nay. She is alone."

He nodded and the buxom young woman led him deeper inside. The cottage was simple but charming like its owner, made of the local stone and of beams and plaster within.

He found Constance in her drying room, engaged in tying bundles of herbs to hang from the rafters. The smells of lavender and sage and other herbs he could not name teased his nostrils. But it was Constance who captured the greater part of his senses. Her gown was blue silk, over a paler silk kirtle. The stiff bodice was richly embroidered with flowers and birds. From her ears hung heavy pearls. Her blonde hair was fashionably braided, still several little curls escaped like wayward thoughts in church.

Her blue eyes sparkled when she saw him and her full lips curved in a smile of welcome. She held out her hands and walked forward with a light step. "Why Rafe, I thought you still in London."

"Business brought me here." He took her hands and kissed each one. "And pleasure. The pleasure of seeing you."

She chuckled and a dimple peeped in her cheeks. "La sir, you flatter me. And is the business that brings you the building of that monstrous great house?"

"In part." She would have pulled her hand away but he held it close against his heart. "When may I have the honor of making you its mistress?"

Her eyelids fluttered and she turned her head away. "In truth, I know not."

"But why? I offer you my name, my heart, all that I am and ever hope to be." His lover was more than ordinarily reluctant. He felt there was some objection he'd yet to uncover. Was he an ass, believing she returned his affection?

"And I am greatly honored. It cannot be, Rafe. Our conditions are too far apart." He felt the quiver in her hands.

"I care not. I love thee."

She turned from him, taking back her hands and her little heels clicked across the wooden floor as she returned to her task. It shielded her countenance but he could see the way her white fingers trembled. When he was with her like this, he could not believe she was indifferent to him. "My heart. What is it?"

3

She paused and a twig of lavender snapped in her hands, sending a spray of tiny buds into the air. Resolutely, she turned again to face him. In a low voice she said, "Rafe, I am not of your kind."

His eyes narrowed slightly on her face. "Are they true then? The rumors?"

Her gaze flew quickly to his, startled, and dropped again. "There are rumors?"

He glanced behind him to the door making certain no one could overhear them. Even so he lowered his voice. To so much as whisper about such things was dangerous. "There are rumors of witchcraft practiced in this house."

The roses in her cheeks bloomed and then faded to pure white, like summer blooms to winter snows in an instant. "This charge is often brought against the lady who lives alone and independent and who has an interest in herbs."

"Tell me truth, Constance. You have nothing to fear from me."

As he had done, she glanced quickly behind him to the door. She came very close to him and, her voice barely above a murmur said, "It is true. I am a witch. That is why I cannot marry you. There could not be a worse wife for you."

He smiled at that. "There could not be a better one. Shall you turn me into a toad if we should disagree? Shall my limbs fall off if I don't pay you the proper attentions?" He was teasing and soon heard her ready chuckle.

"It would be too perilous for you."

"You would be safer married to me. I could offer you my protection. Besides, I have mine own secrets." He smiled slightly. "One does, at court."

"Aye. It is whispered that our fair queen does surround herself with pretty men and that you are a favorite."

"She has been generous to me, but her favor comes with a price. There are certain tasks I am asked to perform."

She seemed to pick up more than he was saying. Was it that quality that made her the most intriguing of any woman he'd ever met? "Are you in danger?"

"I do not think so. But there is a roguish fellow I must meet. He bears certain papers that I must needs put in my own pocket. Once I have secured them I will head back to London and, having presented them to Her Majesty, she will give me leave to return. Then, I hope to carry you to my home as my bride."

"Even after my confession? You still want me?" She seemed almost stunned by his unwavering devotion. She raised her brows at him and her blue eyes danced. "Perhaps I have bewitched you."

He laughed. "That you have, my love."

"I must have some time. I have had no thought of marriage. I must think on it most carefully and consult with my sisters."

While he didn't relish her discussing his proposal with women who were clearly witches, he had to trust her. So he said he would return for her answer in a few weeks.

"Let me offer you some wine and cakes. This morning, Cook was at work on a ginger cake. Your favorite."

And so he had the rare pleasure of an hour with his love and no one else about to distract her. Now that her secret was shared with him she seemed easier, more playful and he was no longer in any doubt as to her feelings. She loved him. He could see it in the way her gaze lingered on his, almost in wonder. The way she spoke of his house and how she longed to see it.

When the time for his meeting grew close, and he rose to take his leave, she put out her hand to clasp his wrist. "Rafe, my heart misgives me. Must you go?"

He kissed the hand that would have held him back. "I must, my heart. Tis a small matter of treason. Proof of a plot to overthrow our fair queen."

"Wait," she said. "Let me make you a protection spell."

He laughed at that. "Here is all the spell I need," he said, and before she could protest, he leaned forward and kissed her ripe lips. They trembled beneath his and then, with a tiny sound, she wrapped her arms around him and returned his embrace.

Picking up his hat, he turned before he was tempted to stay forever, and queen and country be damned.

He strode away quickly, and when he reached the front entrance, he said to Betsy, "Your mistress asked me to send you to her. Adieu." With a quick glance left and right he merged into the dusk.

CHAPTER 2

*R*afe entered Rook Lane and passed swiftly down the ill-smelling thoroughfare. When he reached The Bear Inn, he walked all the way around, his nose quivering like a dog's scenting danger. He saw none and on his next pass, entered the low door of the tavern. "Evening, your lordship," said the oily barman. Rafe had known the rascal since he'd been a young student here himself.

"Evening, Jacob. A tankard of your best ale."

He saw his contact from the most cursory glance around the smoky, low ceilinged room. He was sweating, looking anxiously about with eyes that protruded slightly from his head as though he was always trying to look in all directions. A fearful man. And one who'd betray his own, even if they were murderous spies, for money. Rafe loathed the man on sight.

However, nothing of that showed in his face as he approached the man. "Ah, Jeremiah," he said in his firm voice. "You've letters from my uncle?"

It was the agreed on phrase.

The man swallowed nervously and glanced around, even though Rafe was clearly alone. "Aye," he said at last, his voice high with nerves. "Your uncle Harold is well and God save you, sir."

He sat across from the spy. "Let me see them," he said in a low voice.

With another nervous glance around, the man took an oilskin pouch from an inner pocket and slipped it across the table. Rafe grabbed the guttering candle and brought it close. He wasn't fool enough to take out all the documents, contenting himself with a through perusal of the first.

"I beg you, sir," the nervous man sputtered.

"Peace, fool. I would study the goods before I purchase. Like any good businessman."

There was a low groan. "You'll be the death of me."

"Likely the gallows will," he replied callously. "Treason is punished by hanging, drawing and quartering," he added with relish.

The man's Adam's apple jumped. "But I'm giving you the evidence of a plot against our merciful queen. That is loyalty."

"You do it for the gold, fiend. There's no honor in that."

He couldn't bear to be in the traitor's company any longer. Satisfied that the documents were real and comprehensive, he slipped a smaller pouch from his own pocket and passed it beneath the rough wood table.

He nearly flinched when the man's grasping fingers brushed his before latching onto the purse. Once he had it, Rafe took out a lace-edged handkerchief and wiped his fingers. He could see the man's dilemma. He wanted to count the gold coins, and yet, if he displayed so much wealth in this dim tavern, he might draw unwanted attention.

Rafe smiled sardonically as he rose. "Don't worry, rogue, every gold crown is there. May the devil take thee." And he walked calmly away.

Rafe didn't leave immediately. He'd do nothing to draw attention to himself. He passed a table of rowdy students deep in the cheap beer the rascally landlord kept in barrels. They'd all be ill by morning. He could well remember the violent and predictable results of drinking cheap ale in this inn.

A doxy approached him. Her face was pockmarked and painted and she batted her eyes at him more out of habit than that she had any hope of him. "May I offer you some company, good sir?"

His heart was stirred by pity. He took out a couple of shillings and pressed them into her palm. "Not tonight, good lady. But buy yourself a pie."

"I thank thee," she said almost in wonder. No doubt she'd spend the money on cheap ale, but mayhap she'd manage to get a full meal in her belly. She looked as though she needed one.

Not a single soul showed any interest in him and so he felt it was safe to leave. He was nearly at the door when an unpleasant, nasal voice said, "Why, Sir Rafe. I did not think to find you here. I thought you sitting among the queen's skirts."

Sir Edmund Basson was the last man Rafe wanted to see. He was a gossip, a gambler and he liked to make trouble. Still, he gave the man a hearty handshake and said, "I would not presume to kiss the hem of her skirts."

Sir Edmund was a vile fellow with loose lips and looser

morals, but Rafe knew no harm of him. "What business brings you to Oxford?"

Rafe answered carelessly, "I am building a house in the area."

The man's eyes flashed with malice. "You are too modest, sir. I hear it is not little at all but to be one of the great wonders of Oxfordshire when building is complete."

Rafe laughed heartily. "You know my business rather well Sir Edmund. Pray tell what brings you to Oxford?"

The man shrugged. "Nothing so grand as a building project. I am not so in favor with our queen. I am here merely on some family business."

Rafe didn't care for the man's tone or the calculating look in his eyes. He felt a tingling in his palm as it itched to grab the hilt of his sword. He couldn't indulge himself, though. He had his mission to think of.

He bade Sir Edmund good night and walked out into the night. The weather had grown chill and he pulled his heavy cloak about him. He still scanned carefully ahead, strolling at his ease but always alert.

He longed to return to Harrington Street to bid a proper farewell to Constance and let her know her fears had been groundless, but first he had to rid himself of this treacherous packet of papers. He walked steadily toward the hostelry where he had stabled his horse. He was nearly there when a beggar approached him. He'd seen that beggar before and given him a penny. He shook his head and would have continued on his way but the man stepped in front of him.

He heard footsteps behind him and swung around, his sword already drawn. Sir Edmund closed in on him, a wicked-looking rapier in his hand. Behind him was the still quivering spy who must be quite dizzy from the number of times he had changed his allegiance. Rafe was certain of one thing. This would be the last time.

Another fellow he did not know, who looked to be a common thug or soldier for hire, closed in from the other flank.

Sir Edmund said, "You have something that belongs to me. I'll have it back."

"I'll see you hanged for a traitor."

Sir Edmund gave a low, nasty laugh. "You will not see morning."

His blood began to pound already anticipating the battle. The overwhelming odds against him only sharpened his focus.

Sir Edmund's lip curled in a snarl and he lunged. Rafe threw himself forward, pushing Sir Edmund's blade up with his own, even as he kicked out to the left. He heard the hollow sound of metal on stone as the mercenary's blade hit the ground, buying him a few moments.

Sir Edmund spun out of the way and regained his balance. Once more he attacked, this time more carefully. The two men fought silent, deadly. He saw a slim figure pressed against the stone wall, watching. He wasn't certain, but thought the shape female. A black cat ran past like a liquid shadow.

The mercenary had retrieved his blade and threw himself into the fray. Rafe stepped back, as though dancing with several partners. His footwork was light and sure, but the blade was heavy and sweat was already creeping toward his eyes.

If he killed Sir Edmund, he could soon deal with the

hired blades and so he pressed forward, his arm steady and his intent deadly. The other man was no match for him and soon jumped back yelling, "Take him, ye infernal fools. Earn your gold."

Rafe felt contempt rise in him. "Coward as well as traitor, Sir Edmund?" he said softly, but his words were like lashes.

The other man colored but refused to be drawn. Now the mercenary, with a glance of contempt at the cowardly dandy, lunged at Rafe. He parried and they were soon locked in deadly combat. "Kill him," Sir Edmund shrieked. "Do not stand by idle, man. Make an end of him."

The nervous little man who'd sold him the papers rushed toward him with wavering blade. It gave him a moment's satisfaction to run him through. He fell to the ground with a moan.

He had no time even to wipe his blade before turning back to the mercenary who'd not taken advantage of his inattention. He was surprised. "Obliged to you," he panted, returning to his former fight.

"When a man fights as you do, it should be a fair fight," the man grunted, between the ring of the blades.

The mercenary lunged, leaving his shoulder exposed. Even as Rafe felt the sharp sting of a glancing wound, he hit his mark, forcing his blade deep into the shoulder, rendering the man's sword arm useless. The man fell back, clapping a hand to his shoulder and then shouted, "Behind you."

Too late.

Sir Edmund had moved behind him and Rafe felt the cold steel of betrayal in his back. "The most cowardly cut of all," he said as he fell.

He felt his body turned and was powerless to prevent it.

Hands groped in his doublet, and, though he tried to resist, his strength was waning fast. Sir Edmund withdrew the packet of letters and, pausing only to wipe his sword clean of Rafe's blood, walked back down the road.

He was dying. He regretted not saving his queen, but even more, he regretted not marrying Constance so she'd have the protection of his name, at least. Even if she was a widow. Too late now.

All too late.

CHAPTER 3

Constance could not remain still. She paced. She went to the window and tried to see into the dark night. She sat to her needlework, then rose and paced again. She'd sent her maid to follow Rafe, so strong was her intuition that he was walking into danger. No doubt it was the foolish fancies of a woman in love, but she would rather be foolish than bereft of the only man she'd ever trusted with her secret. The man who would still love her, who would take her as she was.

Her maid should have returned by now. The hour grew late. Now she worried, not only for Rafe, but for Betsy. She heard a cat howl outside her door. She opened it and saw a sleek black cat with golden eyes. It ran in and meowed at her as though shrieking at her to do something. She could sit still no longer. She'd go herself and search for them.

She rang for her coachman, a lusty young country lad named Joseph and ordered her carriage. She wrapped herself in a warm cloak, filled a cloth bag with a few supplies, and then Joseph was at the door. As she was about to step into the carriage, Betsy came running down the road toward her, nearly fainting with the effort. Her breath coming in great gasps, she said, "Sir Rafe, madam. I fear he is killed."

A terrible coldness crept over Constance's limbs. "Take me to him at once," she said, almost dragging the panting girl into the carriage with her. "Where is he? Quickly!"

"On Turl Street. Near the inn."

Joseph didn't need to be told to use all speed. They raced to the scene, tossed about as the coach bumped over the cobbles. A scene of carnage met them. Two men appeared to be dead, one of them was Rafe. He lay on his back, but she knew he lived. A rough looking man leaned over him, pressing some cloth against his chest.

She scrambled from the coach and ran forward dropping to her knees. "Rafe," she cried.

"He's mortally wounded, ma'am," the rough man said. She now saw that he was also wounded. One arm hung useless and he bled from his shoulder.

She saw that he was near the end of his strength and took over, pressing the cloth, already soaked with Rafe's blood. "Rafe," she said, softly. He roused, opening his beautiful, ice-blue eyes and focusing on her face with difficulty.

"I'm sorry, Constance," he said softly. "I fear I shall not have the honor of taking you to wife." He drew a struggling breath. "And I have failed our queen. She is in grave peril."

"Do not speak, my love," she said soothing. "I shall have you comfortable directly."

At her signal, Joseph lifted Rafe's upper body, and, when she and her maid would have taken his feet, the wounded man stopped them. It was he who lifted Rafe's feet. She kept pressing the wound, though the bleeding was sluggish now.

But oh, how much of his life's blood was sliding between the cobblestones.

If they could but get him to her cottage.

She whispered to him, telling him of all the plans she had once they were married. How she'd lay out the gardens of his manor. How she'd decorate his handsome rooms. It was all the stuff of her daydreams, but she felt her voice kept him still with her, even as she felt his life force fading.

Joseph and the wounded man carried him into the cottage, though the commotion caused her neighbors to come out onto the street to see what was going on, or stick their heads out of their windows to peer, as though this were one of Mr. Shakespeare's dramas being acted out by the King's Players.

She had Rafe taken to her own chamber and while her maid lit all the candles, she inspected the wound. It was indeed bad. Not all her arts could save him now.

He grasped her wrist and she felt it was the last of his strength. "The queen. Terrible danger. Must save her."

She touched her hand to his thick, dark hair. His face was growing pale. She wrestled with herself, and then leaned forward. "Rafe. There is a way back. You will be able to save the queen. But you will have a terrible price to pay."

His eyes opened on her, lucid and fierce. "Anything. I care not what the price."

"Rafe, you will be cursed with immortality, doomed to walk the earth in the shadows."

"Must save the Queen," he gasped. "Beg you."

She bowed her head, then kissed his hand, and opened the door to the tall, beautiful woman standing on the other side. "Come in," she said, tears almost choking her.

The woman walked forward into the room.

"I cannot watch," Constance said, and turning, walked blindly out.

"Mistress, the other man needs your help," Betsy said, seeing her distress.

She gave herself a moment only to mourn, then straightened her spine. Time enough to worry about whether she'd done the right thing. Whether her motives were really to save the queen, or whether she'd helped turn Rafe into a creature of the night for her own selfish reasons.

Rafe's unknown helper sat in a chair in the kitchen, a tankard of ale on the scrubbed wooden table in front of him. Betsy had fashioned a crude bandage for his shoulder, and the bleeding seemed to have stopped, but she could read the pain in his countenance.

The black cat was curled in front of the fire as though at home.

She went to the injured man. "I will make you a drink to relieve your pain and prevent fever. And I'll bind the wound for you."

"Much obliged," he said.

RAFE WOKE SLOWLY, waiting for the pain to hit him. He lay perfectly still feeling not pain, but an energy he'd never experienced. It was as though he had accessed some deep underground well of life force. Experimentally, he moved his fingers. They obeyed without a twinge. He steeled himself and then moved one arm. Even the old ache from a past sword fight was absent. He sat up in bed and looked down.

He had felt the stab of that sword from behind and he knew he'd been run through. But no bandage wrapped around him. He had no scar. No pain.

He glanced around the room. It was unfamiliar to him. A bedchamber, but not one he'd ever seen before. He recognized Constance's light sent. Had he died then? No doubt this was hell if he was destined to remember Constance so clearly he could smell her, and yet, never have her near him.

He got out of bed, as agile and spry as a youth. He discovered he still wore his breeches, but of his shirt and doublet there was no sign. A man's robe lay across the chair. It was a dark red silk. He slipped on the robe and opened the door. Constance came forward with her quick, light step as though she had heard him stirring. Though her face broke into a smile, he could see a trace in her eyes of—what? Worry? Fear? She held out both her hands to him. "Rafe. How do you feel?"

What he felt was confused. He took her hands and they felt hot. "What is this place? Are you an angel?"

She laughed at that and her chuckle was so familiar he began to relax. "Nay. I am no angel."

"Then how comes it that I am whole again?"

Her smile faded. "Come. I must explain it all to you."

Vaguely he remembered being near death and desperate to complete his mission. She had promised him she could save him but at a terrible price. Everything was coming back to him now. Yesterday she'd admitted to being a witch. He cared not. He loved her still. But in order to complete his mission she had warned him that he would be turned into a creature he had believed only existed in mythology. "Answer me this. Do I still live?"

She sighed. "I believe the proper term is undead. You neither live as a mortal nor will you die as one. Let me introduce you to your maker. She will explain everything."

He remembered the beautiful woman who had come to him in what he'd believed were his last moments. He'd been drawn to her and frightened of her at the same time. But she had treated him with great kindness. Told him to close his eyes and sleep. The last thing he remembered was her gentle fingers raising his chin.

He felt his eyes widen and his hand slipped up to his throat. Sure enough he felt two tiny indents about the size of sharp teeth. But the wound had already healed.

He had heard of such undead creatures, but not believed they existed.

Constance watched him, looking sad. "I am so sorry. I could not save you. You were too close to death, too badly wounded."

Would he have been quite so desperate to complete his mission at any cost had he realized how high the price would be?

Yes. He knew the answer instantly. He'd been willing to forfeit his life for Queen and country and he'd done it. And gladly. Now he was offered an even greater opportunity. He was gaining power, he could feel it, and again he had that sense of drawing from some deep well. His hearing was so sharp he could hear the scurry of a mouse somewhere up in the attics. He had the strength, now, to complete his mission.

Constance still looked anxious, and he reassured her. "It is well."

She sighed with relief. "Come into the kitchen. Meet the man who helped save you."

His brows rose at that. All he remembered was an ambush. When he walked behind her into the kitchen he checked. The man sitting at his ease with a tankard of ale in front of him was one of those very ruffians who'd attacked him. Automatically he reached for his sword then realized he was not wearing it. He had not even his boots on or any weapon about him.

He glanced around the kitchen, snatching up a knife that sat atop a board containing half a loaf of bread and the remains of a sirloin.

The ruffian who'd been one of his attackers shook his head at him. "Put down your weapon. I mean you no harm. The cut I gave thee was barely a prick."

Rafe suddenly saw the humor in the situation. A laugh rumbled in his chest. "Then I must thank you that it was not your sword that ran me through."

"My sword is for hire anywhere throughout the world. But yet I am an honorable man. I do not hold with cowardly ambushes and those who would stab a man in the back. You have your life back now, and I offer you my services."

Rafe put down the knife. It was too ridiculous to brandish a bread knife at a paid assassin. Especially while wearing a dressing gown of red silk and with his feet bare. "I thank thee," he said with a mock bow. "However, I will not trouble thee."

The man picked up his tankard with his good hand and drank. "As you will. Your secret will remain locked within my breast."

His secret. Rafe had the first inkling that from now on he would have to be a very careful man. No. Not man. Creature.

He glanced behind him to Constance. He had brought trouble to her and her house. Yet she remained calm.

"Constance. What danger have I brought to you? Tell me the truth."

He pulled out a chair for her at the kitchen table and obligingly she sat. He took the one beside her and across from his erstwhile enemy. "You have brought me no danger, Rafe. What threat there is comes from the fear of those who would destroy what they do not understand." She glanced around her own kitchen. At the hanging herbs, and the pot of liquid that hung from its hook over the fire, quietly bubbling. A black cat napped in its warmth. "I have magic. But I use it for good, not ill."

The man across from the table nodded. "And I am mighty grateful for it. It was an evil-tasting brew you gave me last night, but it was a fine strengthening draught. I thank ye."

Rafe reached for Constance's hand. "Do you trust this rascal?" He felt that she saw people more clearly than he could. She nodded. "He is a good man at heart."

"What is your name?"

"I am called William Thresher."

"Then, William Thresher, I will hire thee. Mistress Constance shall be kept safe and her person and property protected. Can you do that?"

"Aye."

"Good. I must go. I've a mission to complete."

Constance stopped him when he would have risen. "Nay. Rafe. You cannot leave here yet. You must wait for Mary. It was she who turned you into what you are. There are rules you must follow. Things you must understand. She will introduce you to others of your kind. It would be treacherous for you out there alone. And you will need a mortal companion. I would that you would take William Thresher with you. Idle tongues will wag if a stranger known to be a man of violence takes up residence here."

In his heart he knew she was right though it pained him to think of leaving her undefended. He could not shake the notion that he had brought danger to her house. If his mission weren't so urgent he would stay and gladly.

As though she had read his mind she said, "You will see Mary tonight. You may be strong enough to leave tomorrow. And you will complete your mission. You will save our queen."

"I vow it."

She turned to William Thresher. "And will you guard your new master with your life?"

William Thresher nodded solemnly. "I pledge you my sword and my life, Sir Rafe. And that of my sons and my sons' sons."

A shiver went through Rafe as he realized that he would be alive to hold this man and his future generations to his promise. But the future could wait. For now he had the small matter of the queen and country to save.

CHAPTER 4

*H*e and Constance spent a very pleasant afternoon together. He wouldn't have believed such a thing was possible, but in silent agreement they did not refer to his changed being or their uncertain future. They spoke as lovers do, of their work, and the improvements he would make to the manor when he brought her home as its mistress. No doubt they both realized how impossible that was now that Sir Edmund knew him for dead.

Just after dusk, Mistress Mary came for him. She seemed to appear. One moment Constance and he had been alone in the front parlor and the next the beautiful redhead with the glittering green eyes stood in front of him. "Come, Rafe. It is time."

He bid Constance adieu and noted that her hand trembled when he kissed it. In a low voice he promised. "I will always come back to you."

Mistress Mary led him back down to the kitchens and behind to a storeroom. He glanced around, wondering why Mary had brought him here. He spied a barrel of ale, a thick round of cheese, eggs and grain that would be milled into flour. She moved toward a barrel that he had believed to contain oil, but she moved it aside with such ease it must be empty. Underneath, a door had been cut into the floor and a metal ring inset. When she pulled on the ring the door lifted and she gestured for him to go first.

He walked down a rough set of steps into a tunnel that was dank and breezy. He heard water running below. Torches burned lighting the stone tunnel and when Mistress Mary had closed the door and stood beside him she shook out her skirts and said, "Welcome to your new home."

"Are there many of us?" He gestured to the burning torches.

"You will discover there are many of us indeed. But we share this underground thoroughfare with the Jews of Oxford. They find it convenient sometimes to stay out of sight, as we do."

They walked a little ways along the passage and she stopped in front of a door that he could easily have walked past. It was set deep into the wall. There was a certain pattern to her knock and then the door was opened by a burly individual who looked suspiciously over Rafe before letting them in.

He found himself in a roomy chamber, well-lit by torches and candles and as luxurious as any nobleman's residence. Thick carpets on the floors, chairs and tables, paintings and tapestries. Everything but windows.

He said, "I cannot stay. I must complete my mission."

"I know," she said in a soothing tone. "But you will not survive without food and safe places to rest during the day."

She led him into a comfortable parlor. A male and

24

female, pale and undead, were sitting talking together and at her look they both rose and left. "Please, sit down."

He did and she explained how he must learn to feed. He did not wish to take a human life but he was hungry and he knew that if he did not feed he would fade away. She laughed away his scruples. "We are not all monsters," she explained. "Fortunately, the medical establishment contains many of us and our friends. Why do you think the practice of cupping is so popular?"

He had never personally been cupped but he knew many people who believed that draining a portion of blood from an ill or injured person helped to heal them. At his look of surprise she nodded. "Much of that lovely blood gets saved and sold to creatures like us. We also have a network of volunteers who let us feed off them directly for a fee. If you are careful and not greedy they come to no harm."

His greatest fear now explained away, he was able to relax and listen to the rest of what she had to tell him. She showed him a secret map and told him that he must memorize it. There he found centers in London and York, Bath and Cambridge. She assured him that there were communities of vampires living in all the large cities of Europe and, indeed, throughout the world. He would learn to recognize his own kind and to live his life in the shadows.

He understood and then asked the question that burned within him. "And Constance?"

Her face grew sad. "Constance is a magical creature, but she is mortal. My spies have been busy and already there is a rumor afoot that you were killed. Constance is already suspected of witchcraft by some in this community. You know how perilous are such whispers. If you appear to rise from the dead and live with her as man and wife..." She made a helpless gesture with her hands and shook her head.

By sunset the next day, Rafe was ready to set out. He'd hired William Thresher a horse and retrieved his own steed and his luggage from the inn he patronized. He tied his black hair back with a leather thong, and carried his hat when he went to bid his love adieu.

Their parting was sweet and sad. When he'd kissed her hand one last time she surprised him by throwing her arms around his neck and kissing him full on the lips. "I love thee," she whispered.

"And I thee."

And then he turned and strode out. He did not look back. He could not.

He and William Thresher rode hard and far into the night. Fortunately there was a full moon to guide them. He felt stronger and more robust than ever in his mortal life but after some hours he recognized that the valiant William Thresher was falling behind. He had to remember that not only was his new servant mortal but he had recently been injured. Still, there was too great an urgency upon him to give the man more than a few hours' rest in a wayside inn.

Sir Edmund had more than a day's advantage.

Rafe had seen enough of those papers to know that the plan was to murder the queen. But he didn't know all the details. Sir Edmund had access to the queen but had already proven himself a coward. Rafe knew it would be others who would do the killing. Sir Edmund would grease their way.

Unless he was prevented.

Grimly, he rode on. A coward could be frightened into telling all he knew. Rafe needed but an hour with the man. Edmund would know when he confronted Rafe that his foe was no longer mortal. He thought he would enjoy acting the monster.

The moon sank and then the veriest hint of dawn lit London's skyline as they rode into town.

There were plenty of rats in London. His job was to nose out one cowardly traitor of a rat and dispose of him like the vermin he was.

CHAPTER 5

Queen Elizabeth was in a mood. Rafe could tell that the moment he stepped into her presence. She was at Richmond Palace, and was usually happiest there. But today she looked discontented and snappish. Her courtiers tried to amuse her, before being waspishly dismissed and wandering away wounded to gossip quietly in the corridors.

It was too cold to hunt. She may have believed Rafe had failed her and her life was again in peril. Elizabeth had been often the target of plots and he doubted if she ever relaxed completely.

As he entered her chamber, he felt curious stares and many of those gossiping fell suddenly silent. From the corner of his eye he saw a lute player make the sign of the cross. He strode forward, refusing to slink away, and when Queen Bess saw him her bored expression lightened immediately. She motioned him forward with an imperious hand. He bent forward in his most graceful bow. "Why, Sir Rafe. They told me you were killed."

He laughed, in what he hoped was a careless fashion. "For shame, Your Majesty. It would take more than death to keep me from worshiping at your feet."

She chuckled and bade him sit beside her. "You're a dog, my dear. But a handsome dog." Her eyes darted quickly about and when she was certain no one was in hearing distance she dropped her voice. "What news?"

"Your spies had good information. There was a plot."

Her sharp green eyes searched his. "And?"

"And there no longer is. Sadly, Your Majesty will not be seeing Sir Edmund Basson at court anymore."

Her painted lips turned down at the corners. "I do not like a traitor. Must I send the bailiff to arrest him?"

"No need. Sir Edmund perished in a sword fight." Rafe had taken satisfaction in running the scoundrel to ground, then defeating him in a sword fight and retrieving the damning evidence, which he had passed on to Sir Francis Walsingham, his queen's trusted spymaster.

"Too easy a death, perhaps."

Perhaps, but Sir Edmund had also provided him a most welcome meal. "But no need for such a plot ever to come to public attention."

She nodded. She was an astute politician and understood better than he did the importance of appearing unassailable. "You have done well, my dear. How may I reward you?"

She was a most generous queen when she was pleased. And he was ready with his request. "I may find it necessary to absent myself from our fair land for some time. I have thoughts of a sea voyage."

Her sharp eyes were steady on his. "You have a taste for adventure."

"I have. But I would keep Crosyer Manor, which Your Majesty was so kind to give me."

She chuckled. "Worried some confounded rogue will snatch it from you when your back is turned? Well, I shall miss you. You're a loyal man and I trust you. I believe this may be a case of the fewer questions asked the better pleased I shall be. I shall have prepared a deed, worded in such a way that the land can never be taken from you or your family."

Which was exactly what he had hoped for. "I thank thee, Your Majesty."

He was grateful to know that his house was his in perpetuity but the true gift Queen Bess had given him was to recognize him. To sit and talk with him. No one in court would now dare treat him any differently than she had. At least, not until his back was turned and they were out from under the watchful eyes of their queen.

He was a peaceable man, but no one could live at court and not fall victim to the various rivalries and jealousies that thrived there. The very fact that his queen did favor him had brought him enemies. Sadly, now that he would be living a shadowed existence, he knew he must be careful to be rarely at court. He had great admiration and love for his queen and would serve her in his own way.

Now that his business was done, he would return to Constance and hope to convince her that a marriage with him while not ideal, was still possible. His changed state had not altered his feelings. He loved her yet and believed his affection was returned.

He returned almost immediately, stopping only at an inn to rest a few hours of an afternoon when the sun was at its height. He made a stop in London on his way back from

Richmond Palace, there to meet with a jeweler and gold-smith. He had in mind a ring for his lady and was shown any number of creations where the goldsmith had shown off his talent with intricate gold work set with rubies, diamonds, pearls, intricately carved Turkey stone and cameos. And yet, Rafe was drawn always back to a simple ring.

It was gold and the setting was subtle rather than elaborate, set with a single, fine ruby.

"It is for a lady, sir?" Goldsmith asked him. When he affirmed that it was, the jeweler said he should engrave a special message. The idea appealed to him. And after some thought he asked for *Amor perpetuo est.*

Love is forever.

SOON HE WAS on his way again. He felt an urgency to be back with Constance. No doubt it was a foolish conceit, the idea that a woman so independent might need him. He suspected the one in need was himself, now he was uncertain of his future and where and how he would live in the world. Perhaps in the time he'd been gone she'd begun to perceive him as a monster and would refuse to see him. And yet, no sooner did he think of Constance than he knew he was being foolish. She was kind and true. Still, the sense of urgency did not leave him and he pushed poor William Thresher almost as hard on the return journey as he had on the way to Richmond.

It came on to rain and the pocked and pitted road became a misery of mud. Still, they trudged on. At last, he spied the tower of Magdalen and knew they were close. Rafe knew his heart would have sped up had his heart not undergone a change like the rest of him and seemed slowed almost to still-ness in his chest.

Still, he urged his tired horse on, splashing through puddles and caring not for the raindrops that dripped from his hat. He wrapped his long coat closer about him. His leather riding boots kept out most of the wet, but not all.

But when he arrived at Constance's cottage there was no cheerful smoke coming from the chimney. The shutters were closed and the knocker off the door. He did not think she had planned a trip.

"Could it be the plague, sir?" William Thresher asked in a low voice.

He shook his head, grim. "No. Look at the markings around the lintel of the door."

William did and said, "Those are the marks of the witch."

A gruff voice from the street called to them. "You'd best go quickly in case the house be spellbound."

He turned and found a stout man looking pugnacious and self-important. "Good sir, I have business here. What has happened to the lady of the house?"

The man shook his head most solemnly. "Nay. That was no lady. That were a witch. My own good wife saw a mortal bad injured fellow carried into that house to die and out he walked again the next morning as stout and strapping as you see me now." He spat. "That woman were in league with the devil."

Since Rafe was held speechless with dread it was William Thresher who asked, "Where has she been taken?"

"To the castle."

William said, "I thank thee, sir."

When the man had passed on, William turned to Rafe. "Good God, what is to be done? I remember when they burned poor Thomas Cramner, the archbishop. I was but a lad. They must not do that to our sweet lady."

"And they shall not." He thought rapidly. He would go and consult with Mary and the other vampires. "You go and find out exactly where she is being held, and who guards her. And who is allowed to visit."

Once William was on his way, Rafe contemplated breaking in but he had no wish to be caught in the process or to damage Constance's home. He tried to form a mental picture of how the tunnels beneath had run. Rook Lane was across the road and when darkness fell he slipped down into the lane. He imagined other buildings must have cellar access into those tunnels. He dropped down into a likely looking stairwell only to stumble into the kitchen of a pub and have a stout cook chase him out, brandishing a heavy saucepan at his head.

He emerged back into Rook Lane and luckily spied two of the vampires who had been with Mistress Mary. He strode quickly up to them and in a low voice asked to be taken to see her.

One looked irritable and impatient. "I was just getting out for a bit of air. I've been cooped up all day."

Rafe stepped closer. He towered above the thin youth, who must have been a student when he was turned. "You'll be worse than cooped up if you don't take me to her immediately."

With a heavy sigh, the young man said, "All right. Follow me."

Two doors down was a discreet door built into the wall.

The youth opened it and the three of them slipped in. Down a set of stairs, through another door and down much cruder steps until he found himself in a disused store room. As in Constance's house there was a barrel set atop a trapdoor and the three of them quickly made their way down to the tunnels. He realized he could easily have gone the wrong way in the labyrinth of archways, and was glad of the escort.

When they reached the vampires' nest beneath Constance's home the other vampire made a certain pattern of knocks upon the wood and once again the heavy door was opened. It was Mistress Mary herself who opened the door and she looked very relieved to see him. "I hoped you'd come."

She beckoned the other two to come inside with him. There were three or four other vampires all gathered in the main parlor. They had a map of Oxford Castle laid out and it was clear they were already planning to rescue Constance. Mary was obviously the leader. She lifted her white bejeweled hand and showed him how they planned to go in as undertakers and bring a supposedly dead Constance out in a coffin.

Rafe hated the plan. He hated the idea of Constance assuming the aspect of death and then being cooped up in a coffin. He shook his head. "Your plan is too complex and too open to mishap."

Mistress Mary raised her eyebrows. "Have you a better plan?"

"I believe boldness may prove more successful than guile." He gave them a rough outline of his idea and they agreed quite readily to help. No doubt because it involved little effort on their part.

Rafe emerged once more aboveground and proceeded to the inn where he had instructed William to hire them rooms. He bathed, dressed himself in the same finery he had worn to court. Much of his plan depended on appearances. William arrived and informed him that Constance's trial was set for three days hence. And that she was being kept in a special witch's cell.

He couldn't bear to think of her in that terrible place but he also couldn't afford to be foolish.

He was acquainted with the governor of the castle but slightly. The man was known by repute to enjoy a heavy dinner and then retire of an afternoon to his gentle repose. Therefore, Rafe timed his visit so he arrived just as the man was enjoying the last of his afternoon repast.

Rafe knew he would not be denied his meeting given his connection with court and so it turned out. He was ushered into the governor's private quarters. The governor was a fat, indolent man. The remains of a hearty meal sat in front of him. He had grease about his mouth and a glass of claret in his hand.

"Sir Rafe, this is indeed a pleasure." He took in Rafe's court dress and said, "Join me in a glass of claret."

Rafe nodded and was soon seated across from his host sipping the red wine sparingly. The large man yawned and Rafe felt he must discharge his deed quickly before his host fell asleep under his eyes. "I believe you hold a woman here by the name of Constance Mayhew."

The governor shook his head, looking solemn. "Not a woman, Sir Rafe. A witch. She worships the devil and has been seen cavorting with demons."

Rafe remained calm with an effort. "I am here by order of Her Majesty."

That startled the man into opening his eyes wide. "I hope our fair queen enjoys her customary good health?"

"Indeed, but she has a...waiting woman who suffers a trifling complaint about her hands." He dropped his tone. "Warts."

He waited for the man's expression of distaste to pass.

"Good Queen Bess would see her waiting woman cured of this ailment. She has heard that Mistress Constance has a great talent for curing the sad affliction. She would have her escorted to Richmond Palace, there to minister to the waiting woman."

The man did not look happy. "But her trial is set. She must be investigated. What will our glorious queen do with a witch once she has fulfilled her dark purpose?"

Rafe drew himself up cold and severe. "Ours is not to question Her Majesty."

The man babbled to excuse himself. "No, no. Only I must consult. Where is your authorization? Where is your order from the Queen?"

Rafe looked down at the greasy man as he would a beetle crawling across the filthy floor. "Do you think Her Majesty would put such an order in writing? Fool. This is a matter the most secret."

The governor was sweating profusely now, clearly unsure of his safest course. Rafe felt for him. Surely the rabble longing for a witch's trial would be sorry to be denied their pleasure, but should he dare disobey the Queen his future looked very dim indeed.

Rafe watched him wrestling with his options and finally

he said, "Fine. I trust your word as a gentleman. But you cannot take her now. It must be done under cover of darkness else there may be a riot. Folks do not like to see a witch go free."

Thus it was arranged that Rafe would come to collect Mistress Constance that night at ten of the clock. He was not to come through the main gate but by the back entrance used by the servants and gaolers. Much as he longed to get Constance out of this stinking place immediately, he bowed his head as though the matter were of little importance and left the man to his afternoon sleep.

CHAPTER 6

The horses' hooves echoed off the cobbled streets and a dank mist drifted from the river as Rafe and William approached the back entrance of the castle. It loomed dark and impenetrable. He had expected to find Constance waiting there with one or two keepers but instead there were six large, rough-looking men waiting. His horse twitched and beside him William made a movement for his sword but Rafe stopped him, even as his own sword arm itched for action. In a low voice he said, "If this be a trap, you know what to do."

Then he rode on. When he reached the group one stepped forward who appeared to be its leader. He was a rough looking character with a badly-pocked face and a scar from a sword dragging down his mouth.

"I am here on the Queen's business," he said softly. "My name is Sir Rafe Crosyer."

The man gave a loud laugh. "The devil's business more like. You was mortally wounded. I seen you with my own eyes outside The Bear. Then you was taken to that witch's house and now look at you." The man spat. "Oh, you'll see your mistress all right. And you'll both go to the devil, your master."

And then he was surrounded. He was grabbed from his horse and pulled down. Between them, he and William could have made short work of these six ruffians, but they chose, instead, to let him be taken. He said, "Let me go, in the name of Her Majesty."

"Your Majesty is the devil and well do I know it." The ruffian grabbed Rafe's sword and as the six men bundled him in through the back entrance William wheeled his horse around and galloped off into the night.

They dragged him down a set of stone steps to a narrow arched corridor. It was ill lit and very cold. He wondered how anyone survived being incarcerated down here. Poor Constance. He never should have left her. It was his fault she was here.

They dragged him to the end of the passage. One of the men pulled out a ring of keys and opened a rough door and then shoved him through. Stumbling forward, he found himself in a small stone room. There was no light but that coming from a single tallow candle sitting atop a rough wooden table. A straw pallet was thrown in the corner and on this Constance sat, shivering.

"My heart. What have they done to you?"

"Rafe," she cried out in a soft voice, struggling to rise.

He ran to her. "Oh my poor love. Have they hurt you?"

"No." And then her smile wobbled. "Not yet."

"Nor shall they."

He took his heavy cloak from around his shoulders and wrapped it around her slim body. He only wished he had more body warmth to share. Still, he wrapped his arms around her for support if not warmth.

She said, "You should not have come. Now you are doomed, too."

He smiled, briefly. "You are not friendless. We have a plan to get you out."

In a tart voice that showed her spirit returning as her body warmed she said, "No magic is that strong."

He withdrew a leather sack from an inner pocket. "Not magic. Black powder."

When her eyebrows rose in silent question he said, "Gunpowder."

"Is it not dangerous?"

"Very. This will either give us our escape or a quick death."

She nodded. "A fair bargain."

He chose a spot in the middle of the cell and piled the gunpowder into a black mound.

She said, "That does not seem a great deal of powder. Is not the floor very thick?"

"You're quite right, my love. This is merely for the signal. The bulk of the gunpowder is below us. As I said, you have loyal friends."

"Who would blow me to kingdom come."

He glanced up at her. "Ready?"

She nodded slowly. He went to her. Kissed her once. And told her to tuck herself into the farthest corner of the cell.

He took the sputtering candle, put it into the gunpowder and then threw himself into the corner, arching his body over Constance's.

He smelled the acrid smell of burning and then the

gunpowder exploded. Barely had the sound stopped ringing than a much greater explosion sounded below their feet. Oh how he hoped that map had been accurate and his knowledge of explosives correctly remembered.

It felt as though the earth moved and he wondered if the entire castle would cave in upon them. A chunk of stone hit him in the shoulder, and bits of sand and pebbles rained down on them. Then the world ceased to shake and he turned his head. A jagged hole had appeared in the bottom of the cell.

Already, he could hear shouts from other parts of the prison. He hauled a stunned looking Constance to her feet and propelled her forward to the gaping hole. A rough ladder appeared and he handed her down to the waiting vampires, then climbed down behind her.

Mistress Mary was holding Constance in her arms and over her head their gazes met. Mary's was one of wintry approval.

He looked behind him and saw a crew of three stone masons all ready to begin the repair. Mary said, "We created a few other diversions in the prison. Besides, the gaolers are too frightened of the witch to enter her cell lest she cast evil spells on them. It will be morning before anyone notices her gone and by that time the floor will be repaired. No one will ever know how she escaped." She shrugged her elegant shoulders. "They'll assume witchcraft."

He was glad these undead creatures would not be discovered. "You'll be safe enough, then."

EVEN WITH THE whole night ahead of them, they could not waste a minute. He said gently, "Come, my love."

Constance looked at him and her hair gleamed gold in the torchlight. "Where, Rafe? Where can we go that is safe?"

"We ride to Scotland."

"Scotland?"

"Aye. You have friends there. Sisters."

"Shall I ever return?"

She was tired and cold and frightened. He stroked a smudge of dust off her face. "Perhaps."

CHAPTER 7

$\mathcal{W}$illiam Thresher was waiting at the crossroad with fast horses. Rafe took Constance up with him and they rode, the three of them, all through the night. They changed horses at post houses along the route. Constance was uncomplaining of the long hours in the saddle. They stayed in out-of-the way inns, giving different names at each stop. William Thresher posed as the master, Constance his sister, and Rafe their servant. They rode for three grueling days and when, at last, they reached Edinburgh, Constance was slumped against him with fatigue.

She brightened, however, as they rode in. "Why Edinburgh is beautiful."

Rafe was sorry he could not take his bride to the manor house he'd built with her in mind. However, they settled in a pretty cottage. William remained as their servant. They married quietly and lived happily. Their comfort increased when William married a local woman and fathered a large and noisy family. For many years they were happy.

But Constance aged and Rafe didn't. He was a scholar,

known to work so diligently that he was never seen during the strongest hours of sunlight. Constance's magic was strong, but not strong enough to make Rafe appear to age. When she was more than fifty years of age and he still looked thirty-five, people began to whisper.

There had been witch trials in Edinburgh too and Constance and her secret coven had to be very careful. She went to them, asking for help. She and Rafe had agreed they must move somewhere else, but where would be safe?

Constance had a sister who had married the youngest son of a baron and sailed to America where the family had lands. One of the oldest and gentlest of women said, "You must go to your sister, across the sea to America."

"America. So far?" She remembered when Scotland had seemed a distant land. But to cross an ocean?

"Many of our kind have already fled there. I myself have daughters and nieces settled happily at a place named Salem in Massachusetts. They tell me the land is bountiful, and the air healthful."

And so they set sail for America.

Constance was joyfully reunited with her sister, now a widow, and a baby niece, who lived with them. She found a new family of witches there and added to her knowledge of herbs and healing. There was a great deal to learn from the native peoples.

Constance's sister died, but her daughter grew strong and healthy and as beautiful as her mother and her aunt. She was also a gifted witch.

The New World was in some ways more forgiving than the old. If Constance had a much younger and very handsome husband who should blame her? They enjoyed twenty happy years there. They saw their niece married and settled.

Constance passed away, a happy and fulfilled woman, but her great sorrow was that she and Rafe must be parted.

Once his beloved wife was gone he knew a time of despair.

He wandered, then, to all parts of the globe. However, every century or so when he could be certain no one alive remembered him, he would return to Oxford. He would walk down Harrington Street and recall the happy times he'd spent at Constance's cottage. He'd spend time at his manor, which he'd managed to hold onto for most of its history.

More than half a millennium passed. Rafe was a scholar still, teaching sometimes at his old college, Cardinal College, and working as a consultant for the Bodleian Library. He was living at his manor house and William, the many times descendant of his loyal servant William Thresher, looked after his needs and kept his secrets.

He'd been in Italy, inspecting some illuminated manuscripts on behalf of the Bodleian. Whenever he returned to Oxford, he liked to stop in at Cardinal Woolsey's knitting and yarn shop. It was built on the site that had once held Constance's cottage and he'd become friendly with Agnes Bartlett, the woman who owned the shop. He was looking forward to catching up on all the gossip he'd missed.

He glanced ahead and saw a sight that made him stop dead in his tracks. Nearly stumble in fact. "Constance?" He mouthed the word for he knew it could not be she, and yet, his poor ancient heart yearned. The woman walking towards him had the same long curly blond hair, the bright blue inquisitive eyes, and heart-shaped face. She was dressed like a modern girl of her era, however, in jeans and boots and a casual coat. She dragged a suitcase behind her on wheels.

To his amazement, she turned towards Cardinal Woolsey's. Before she caught him staring like a fool he quickly turned away down Rook Lane.

He recalled now that Agnes had said her granddaughter was coming to visit. But how was it possible that Agnes Bartlett's granddaughter was the image of his long dead and most beloved wife?

He should leave now. If he had any sense, he'd pack up and move somewhere he hadn't lived in a while. Switzerland perhaps, or Canada.

But the thought was no sooner formed then dismissed. He'd let Agnes and her granddaughter get reacquainted. Much later, he'd pay Agnes a visit and perhaps he'd make the acquaintance of that granddaughter. What was her name again? Lucy. That was it.

Lucy.

A Note from Nancy

Dear Reader,

Thank you for reading *Tangles and Treason*, the Vampire Knitting Club's prequel. I am so grateful for all the enthusiasm this series has received.

I hope you'll consider leaving a review and please tell your friends who like cozy mysteries. You can review *Tangles and Treason* on Amazon or Goodreads.

Your support is the wool that helps me knit up these yarns. Turn the page for a sneak peek of *The Vampire Knitting Club*, Book 1.

Until next time,
Happy Reading,

Nancy

THE VAMPIRE KNITTING CLUB

CHAPTER 1

Cardinal Woolsey's knitting shop has appeared on postcards celebrating the quaint views of Oxford, of which there are many. But when a visitor has tired of writing 'wish you were here' on the back of pictures of the various colleges, the dreaming spires, and the dome of the Radcliffe Camera, a cozy little shop painted blue, brimming with baskets of wool and hand-knit goods, can be so much more inviting.

My grandmother Agnes Bartlett owned the knitting shop and I was on my way to visit after spending a very hot month at a dig site in Egypt visiting my archeologist parents.

Gran was always ready to wrap her warm arms around me and tell me everything was going to be all right. I needed comforting after discovering my boyfriend of two years Todd had stuck his salami in someone else's sandwich. I referred to him now as my ex-boyfriend The Toad. I was thinking about Gran's wisdom, her hugs and her home made gingersnaps, when I started to feel as though cold, wet fingers were walking down the back of my neck.

My wheeled suitcase clanked and rattled behind me along the cobblestones of Harrington Street as I looked around, wondering what had caused the heebie-jeebies.

The October day was chilly and crisp and, in the mid-afternoon, the street was busy with shoppers, tourists and students. Church bells chimed three o'clock. When I glanced ahead, I saw my beloved Gran. She wore a black skirt, sensible shoes and one of her hand-knit cardigans, this one in orange and blue. She was walking with a glamorous woman in her sixties whom I didn't recognize. I thought Gran looked confused and my hackles immediately rose. The glamor puss was holding an umbrella over Gran's head, even though the day was dry and there wasn't a cloud in the sky.

I waved and called, "Gran!" moving faster so my suitcase began to bounce.

I was sure they saw me, but as I sped toward them, they veered down a side street. What on earth? I lifted my case and began to run; though my case was so heavy it was more of a grunting stagger.

"Gran!" I yelled again. I stopped at the bottom of the road where I'd last seen them. There was no one there. A dry, shriveled leaf tumbled toward me and from a window ledge a small, black cat regarded me with what looked like pity. Otherwise, the street was empty.

"Agnes Bartlett!" I yelled at the top of my lungs.

I stood, panting. The side street was lined with a mixture of half-timbered cottages and Victorian row houses, all clearly residential. Gran hadn't popped into a shop and would soon emerge. She was visiting in one of those homes, presumably. I wondered if it belonged to her friend.

Well, there was no point standing there. I'd go to Cardinal Woolsey's and wait for Gran there. Her assistant, Rosemary, would be running the shop and I could let myself into the upstairs flat and unpack while I waited for my grandmother to return.

I retraced my steps, but when I reached the entrance to the quaint shop and tried the door, it didn't open. I tried again, pushing harder, before my other senses kicked in and I realized that no lights were on inside.

A printed sign hung on the windowed front door. It said, "Cardinal Woolsey's is closed until further notice." At the bottom was a phone number.

Closed until further notice?

Gran never closed the shop outside her regular closing days. And if she had, where was her assistant?

I stood on the sidewalk that feeling came again, like cold fingers on the nape of my neck.

Order your copy today! *The Vampire Knitting Club* is Book 1 in the Vampire Knitting Club series.

Turn the page to see more books by Nancy.

ALSO BY NANCY WARREN

The best way to keep up with new releases, plus enjoy bonus content and prizes is to join Nancy's newsletter at NancyWarrenAuthor.com or join her in her private FaceBook group Nancy Warren's Knitwits.

Vampire Knitting Club: Paranormal Cozy Mystery

Lucy Swift inherits an Oxford knitting shop and the late-night knitting club vampires who live downstairs.

Tangles and Treason - A free prequel for Nancy's newsletter subscribers

The Vampire Knitting Club - Book 1

Stitches and Witches - Book 2

Crochet and Cauldrons - Book 3

Stockings and Spells - Book 4

Purls and Potions - Book 5

Fair Isle and Fortunes - Book 6

Lace and Lies - Book 7

Bobbles and Broomsticks - Book 8

Popcorn and Poltergeists - Book 9

Garters and Gargoyles - Book 10

Diamonds and Daggers - Book 11

Herringbones and Hexes - Book 12

Ribbing and Runes - Book 13

Mosaics and Magic - Book 14

Cat's Paws and Curses - A Holiday Whodunnit

Vampire Knitting Club Boxed Set: Books 1-3

Vampire Knitting Club Boxed Set: Books 4-6

Vampire Knitting Club Boxed Set: Books 7-9

Vampire Knitting Club Boxed Set: Books 10-12

Vampire Knitting Club: Cornwall: Paranormal Cozy Mystery

Boston-bred witch Jennifer Cunningham agrees to run a knitting and yarn shop in a fishing village in Cornwall, England—with characters from the Oxford-set *Vampire Knitting Club* series.

The Vampire Knitting Club: Cornwall - Book 1

Village Flower Shop: Paranormal Cozy Mystery

In a picture-perfect Cotswold village, flowers, witches, and murder make quite the bouquet for flower shop owner Peony Bellefleur.

Peony Dreadful - Book 1

Karma Camellia - Book 2

Highway to Hellebore - Book 3

Luck of the Iris - Book 4

Vampire Book Club: Paranormal Women's Fiction Cozy Mystery

Seattle witch Quinn Callahan's midlife crisis is interrupted when she gets sent to Ballydehag, Ireland, to run an unusual bookshop.

Crossing the Lines - Prequel

Great Witches Baking Show: Paranormal Culinary Cozy Mystery

Poppy Wilkinson, an American with English roots, joins a reality show to win the crown of Britain's Best Baker—and to get inside Broomewode Hall to uncover the secrets of her past.

Abigail Dixon: 1920s Cozy Historical Mystery

In 1920s Paris everything is très chic, except murder.

Death of a Flapper - Book 1

Toni Diamond Mysteries

Toni Diamond is a successful saleswoman for Lady Bianca Cosmetics in this series of humorous cozy mysteries.

Frosted Shadow - Book 1

Ultimate Concealer - Book 2

Midnight Shimmer - Book 3

A Diamond Choker For Christmas - A Holiday Whodunnit

Toni Diamond Mysteries Boxed Set: Books 1-4

The Almost Wives Club: Contemporary Romantic Comedy

An enchanted wedding dress is a matchmaker in this series of romantic comedies where five runaway brides find out who the best men really are.

The Almost Wives Club: Kate - Book 1

Secondhand Bride - Book 2

Bridesmaid for Hire - Book 3

The Wedding Flight - Book 4

If the Dress Fits - Book 5

The Almost Wives Club Boxed Set: Books 1-5

Take a Chance: Contemporary Romance

Meet the Chance family, a cobbled together family of eleven kids who are all grown up and finding their ways in life and love.

Chance Encounter - Prequel

Kiss a Girl in the Rain - Book 1

Iris in Bloom - Book 2

Blueprint for a Kiss - Book 3

Every Rose - Book 4

Love to Go - Book 5

The Sheriff's Sweet Surrender - Book 6

The Daisy Game - Book 7

Take a Chance Boxed Set: Prequel and Books 1-3

For a complete list of books, check out Nancy's website at
NancyWarrenAuthor.com

ABOUT THE AUTHOR

Nancy Warren is the USA Today Bestselling author of more than 100 novels. She's originally from Vancouver, Canada, though she tends to wander and has lived in England, Italy, and California at various times. While living in Oxford she dreamed up The Vampire Knitting Club. Favorite moments include being the answer to a crossword puzzle clue in Canada's National Post newspaper, being featured on the front page of the New York Times when her book *Speed Dating* launched Harlequin's NASCAR series, and being nominated three times for Romance Writers of America's RITA award. She has an MA in Creative Writing from Bath Spa University. She's an avid hiker, loves chocolate, and most of all, loves to hear from readers! The best way to stay in touch is to sign up for Nancy's newsletter at NancyWarrenAuthor.com or www.facebook.com/groups/NancyWarrenKnitwits

To learn more about Nancy and her books
NancyWarrenAuthor.com

Printed in Great Britain
by Amazon

37604374R00040